Published by Scholastic Inc.
90 Old Sherman Turnpike, Danbury, Connecticut 06816.

For information regarding permission, write to:
Disney Licensed Publishing
114 Fifth Avenue, New York, New York 10011.

ISBN 0-7172-6805-5

Designed and produced by Bill SMITH STUDIO.

Printed in the U.S.A.
First printing, October 2003

Don't Stop Now!

A Story About
Persistence

by **Kristen Behrens &
Monique Peterson**
illustrated by
S.I. International

SCHOLASTIC INC.

New York   Toronto   London   Auckland   Sydney
Mexico City   New Delhi   Hong Kong   Buenos Aires

"*A*ttention!" Captain Li Shang called.
"Yao! Ling! Chien-Po! Ping! Step forward!"

The four soldiers lined up and saluted as their names were called. Even the captain didn't know that the boy named Ping was Mulan in disguise.

"Today you will compete in a challenge," the captain said. "You must bring back all four flags before the sun sets. You have half an hour to get ready."

Breathless, Mulan ran to her tent. "Oh, Mushu," she said. "I hope our group can complete the entire challenge."

"You won't be the first to complete it if you are the last to leave," Mushu said, reminding Mulan she needed to hurry.

"You're right," Mulan agreed and rushed outside. As she did, her foot hit a tent pole.

Flop! The entire tent fell down. Mulan desperately tried to fix it. "Oh, I don't have time!" she said. "I have to go!" She ran to join her team.

"Don't worry about me!" said Mushu, his voice muffled by canvas. "I'm used to fixing everyone else's problems. That's what I'm here for."

The gong sounded. It was time for Mulan's group to move out.

"Don't worry, Captain," she called. "We'll be the first group to bring back all four flags."

The captain just smiled.

Yao glared at Mulan. "Why did you say that, Ping? You know that all the other groups have said that the fourth flag is impossible to get."

"Impossible for them, maybe. But not for us," Mulan boasted.

"*I*'m not so sure," Ling said. He scratched his skinny chin.

"I am," said Mulan. "As long as we work hard and work together, we can do anything!"

Large, yet gentle, Chien-Po nodded in agreement.

"*H*ere's the first flag," Ling said excitedly. "Look." He pointed at a huge boulder.

Chien-Po, Ling, Mulan, and Yao put their backs to the boulder and tried to push it off the flag. But the boulder wouldn't budge.

"This is impossible," Ling said dejectedly.

Mulan thought hard. "I have an idea!" she said.

Mulan ran back along the trail and returned with a long branch she had seen earlier.

"With a lever, we can lift anything," she said.

Mulan, Ling, and Chien-Po lifted the rock off the flag. Yao quickly pulled the flag out from beneath the boulder.

"We did it!" Ling said triumphantly.

"That wasn't so hard," Yao said.

Mulan smiled.

"*I* see the second flag," Yao suddenly exclaimed.

Chien-Po, Ling, and Mulan looked around. "Where?" they asked.

Yao pointed up.

Mulan quickly climbed the tree. But the branch was too thin to carry her weight, so she tried shaking it instead. Sadly, the flag was tied too tightly.

"How could the other groups get this one down?" Yao asked. "No one's as light as Ping." Mulan looked around. A tree branch had helped them before. What could help them now? "I know!" she exclaimed.

*T*hey tugged a long vine out of the shrubbery. Mulan formed it into a lasso and handed it to Yao. "Here, use this," she said.

Yao lassoed the branch and pulled it to the ground. Ling grabbed the flag.

"See? We *can* do this," Mulan said proudly.

*T*he group marched swiftly along the trail, singing as they went.

Suddenly Chien-Po cried, "Oh no—look!"

"Let's lift Ping up to the ledge," Yao suggested. Mulan's fellow soldiers hoisted her up to a ledge. Unfortunately, she wasn't tall enough to reach the ledge above her.

"All of us have to get up here," she said. "Help me back down. I have a plan."

Ling, Mulan, and Yao groaned as Chien-Po used their backs as stepping stones to reach the ledge.

Mulan then looked up at Chien-Po. "You're so strong, now you can pull us all up."

Once Chien-Po had lifted everyone to the next ledge, the others formed another pyramid. Chien-Po stepped on their backs to reach the next ledge. Then he lifted the others up again.

$\mathcal{F}$inally, they reached the highest ledge. With a shout, Ling grabbed the flag.

"We did it again!" Mulan cried.

"Yes!" Yao exclaimed. "Now all we have to do is get back down!"

$\mathcal{A}$t last, they made it down the mountain, huffing and puffing.

"Just one more flag to go," Mulan said.

"I don't think we can do it," Ling said tiredly.

"We can't give up now," Mulan replied.

"There it is!" shouted Mulan. The next flag lay across a rushing river.

"This one's easy," Yao said. "We just have to swim across."

"No," Mulan said. "The current's too strong. And look!" She pointed to a roaring waterfall just downstream.

Chien-Po sat down to think. "Ouch," he said. He stood up, pulling a splinter of bamboo from the seat of his pants.

"That gives me an idea!" Mulan said. "We can build a bridge."

"A bridge—with what?" Chien-Po asked.

"With bamboo," said Mulan.

The tired friends cut pieces of bamboo and tied them together with vines. After a long time, they finally had something they thought was long enough and strong enough to cross the river.

Working together, they tried to extend one end to the other side of the river . . . but it didn't reach!

Chien-Po, Ling, and Yao slumped over.
"We're wet, tired, and hungry," they said.
"Can we go back to camp now, Mulan?"

She looked at her friends. They had done
just as well as the
other groups.

Mulan sighed. They were so close to getting the fourth flag.

What would a princess do?

Mulan pointed at the sun. "There's still time," she said. "We can't give up now. Besides, we might face more difficult challenges when we meet our enemy. We have to know that no matter what happens we can get the job done!"

"You're right. Let's do it!" Chien-Po, Ling, and Yao exclaimed.

*W*orking quickly, they cut more bamboo and double-tied it onto the first bridge. Ling tested the bridge to make sure it would hold Mulan.

Finally, the bridge was finished. Mulan crawled across and snatched the final flag.

Breathless, they ran back to the camp. Each proudly waved a flag.

The gong sounded and they all lined up before Captain Li Shang.

He looked at each of them and smiled. "Well done, men."

"You're the best friends a gir-uh-guy could have!" Mulan said.

"We could never have done it without your encouragement and persistence, Ping," said Ling.

"That's right," Chien-Po and Yao agreed. "Thanks to you, we didn't give up."

Mulan returned to her tent, exhausted but very happy.

"You look like something the cat dragged in," said Mushu.

"I've had a really tough day," Mulan said.

"*You've* had a tough day?" Mushu asked.

"I spent all day trying to fix this tent."

Mulan looked at the crooked tent. "Thanks. It's nice to know I can count on you."

"You got that straight—even if the tent isn't," Mushu said. Just as Mulan fell asleep, she heard Mushu add, "You can always count on your number one dragon!"

The End